My Cat Maisie

For Bridie and Andrew

Viking
Penguin Books Australia Ltd
487 Maroondah Highway, PO Box 257
Ringwood, Victoria 3134, Australia
Penguin Books Ltd
Harmondsworth, Middlesex, England
Viking Penguin Inc.
40 West 23rd Street, New York, NY 10010, USA
Penguin Books Canada Limited
2801 John Street, Markham, Ontario, Canada, L3R 1B4
Penguin Books (N.Z.) Ltd
182-190 Wairau Road, Auckland 10, New Zealand

First published by Penguin Books Australia, 1990

1 3 5 7 9 10 8 6 4 2

Designed by Deborah Brash/Brash Design
Typeset in Berling Roman by Amazing Faces
Made and printed in Hong Kong through Bookbuilders Limited

CIP

Allen, Pamela.
My cat Maisie.

ISBN 0 670 83251 0.

1. Cats -- Juvenile fiction. I. Title

A823.3

My Cat Maisie

Pamela Allen

VIKING

Once upon a time there was a little boy called
Andrew who didn't have anyone to play with.
The big boy next door had a dog called Lobo
but Andrew didn't have anyone.

One morning when Andrew was doing nothing in particular he heard a scr-atch, scr-at-ch, s-c-r-a-t-c-h, at the door.

'I wonder what that can be?' said Andrew.

'I didn't hear anything,' said his mother.

'There's someone at the door,' said Andrew.

'It's far too early for anyone to call,' said his mother.

'It might be someone special,' said Andrew. 'Come on, let's open the door and see.'

When Andrew opened the door,
there was a stray cat.
A very scruffy ginger cat.
'She wants to come in,' said Andrew.

'I wonder if she'd like a drink?' said
Andrew's mother.
Andrew gave her a saucer of milk and
she lapped it up to the very last drop.

'Will you stay and be my cat?' said Andrew.

'I know lots of marvellous games we can play,'
and he gave her a great big hug.

'Let's play wild Indians and you can be the horse,' said Andrew.

'Let's be helicopters and whizz round and round.

Let's be fire engines and go oooOOOOOOoooooOOOooo!

Let's be acrobats and do amazing tricks.'

But the cat wouldn't stay.
Andrew ran after her.
'Please don't go,' he called.

The cat squeezed under the gate and was gone.
Andrew followed.
He climbed over the gate,

and there was Lobo all by himself.
'Have you seen my cat?' said Andrew.

Lobo was so pleased to see him that he
licked his face all over.
'Stop it Lobo!'
But Lobo took no notice at all.
He licked and licked and licked some more.

Lobo wanted to play.
He knew lots of marvellous games, so he
gallumphed all over Andrew.

He was so excited he was silly.
He barked and barked and barked.

He wanted to play leaping, jumping and pushing.

He wanted to play chasing and catching.

Andrew didn't stay.
He climbed back over the gate,

ran up the path and inside
the house as fast as he could.

'The cat wouldn't stay,' blurted Andrew,
'and Lobo's too BIG AND ROUGH!'

His mother gave him a warm
understanding hug.

That night Andrew was feeling sad and lonely
when he heard a scr-atch, scr-at-ch, s-c-r-a-t-c-h
at the window.
Who could that be?

'My cat!' exclaimed Andrew.
When he opened the window she leapt onto the bed.
'This time I've come to stay,' she seemed to say.
Andrew stroked her gently, very very gently.

'I'll call you Maisie,' murmured Andrew,
and Maisie began to wash herself.

'And you can sleep on my bed whenever
you want to,' said Andrew.
Maisie washed herself some more,

then snuggled up close,
curled herself into a ball,
and purred, and purred, and purred.